Margaret's First Holy Week

The story of a stray that was born
on the Via della Conciliazione in Rome
and is adopted by the Pope, and how she then runs the
Vatican from museum to floorboard. For ages six and up.

THE POPE'S CAT SERIES

This volume is preceded by

The Pope's Cat

Margaret's Night in St. Peter's (A Christmas Story)

Coming next

Margaret and the Pope Go to Assisi

Margaret's First Holy Week

JON M. SWEENEY
Illustrated by ROY DELEON

PARACLETE PRESS

BREWSTER, MASSACHUSETTS

Ⴑ   Δ

2019 First Printing
Margaret's First Holy Week

Text copyright © 2019 Jon M. Sweeney
Illustrations copyright © 2019
by Roy DeLeon

ISBN 978-1-61261-937-8

This is a work of fiction. The author
has used the real titles of Pope and Holy
Father in the sense in which they are normally
understood: for the leader of the Roman Catholic
Church who resides in Vatican City; but no historical
Pope or Holy Father, past or present, is intended.

Published by Paraclete Press
Brewster, Massachusetts
www.paracletepress.com

Printed in Canada

To the child in all of us
—Jon

To my Benedictine family at St. Placid Priory
—Roy

Snore! The Pope heard Margaret the second he walked into the apartment. He was just returning from morning Mass in his private chapel.

Margaret was curled up in a ball on the couch by the window, her head resting on palm branches the Pope left there a few days ago after the long, joyful procession through St. Peter's Square on Palm Sunday.

Margaret was exhausted. Cats are often, you know, exhausted!

It has been nearly a year since the Pope adopted Margaret, and Margaret adopted the Pope. They live together in the Pope's apartments in Vatican City, the tiniest country on earth.

The Swiss Guards, who protect the Pope, long ago learned to open doors for Margaret. The Pope's friends long ago began to regard her as one of the family. But . . . it is still true . . . there are some members of the Curia—people at the Vatican who help the Pope in his official work—who are not happy that Margaret is around. They believe the Pope is too important a person to be walking around with a cat.

And Margaret . . . well . . . she sometimes gets into trouble.

The palm branches that Margaret had been comfortably resting on were all that remained in the apartment, and the Vatican, from the celebrations of Palm Sunday. Margaret loved that day, watching people clap their hands and wave their palm fronds, and then the happy Mass. She especially enjoyed singing songs about Jesus the king.

But that was five days ago.

Today was Thursday. Margaret was waking up to the fifth day of Holy Week, and she could already tell that the feeling in the Vatican was changing.

While she stretched herself out of her slumber, Margaret heard the Pope talking with someone in the apartment. Father Felipe, the Pope's secretary, had come into the room. They were using a strange-sounding word—it was nothing she had ever heard in English or Italian. "*Tenebrae*" (pronounced *ten-e-bray*), she heard them each say.

"Darkness" and "shadows," Felipe said, as well.

That's what *Tenebrae* means. It is a church service that takes place as Holy Week moves toward Easter, when the church is made completely dark. Margaret's ears perked up.

Is it scary? she wondered.

Then the Pope said, "This is one time when everyone should leave with a sense of sadness." *Oh my!* Margaret thought. She was worried.

Tenebrae is a Latin word, and it means just what Margaret heard. It isn't scary, but it *is* supposed to be sort of sad. Holy Week begins with the joyful celebration and procession that remembers Jesus arriving in Jerusalem on the first Palm Sunday more than 2,000 years ago, but then gradually moves toward his Passion.

Margaret didn't know what "Passion" meant. Not yet.

Father Felipe then left the room, and the Pope noticed that Margaret was finally awake. He picked her up, pressing his cheek to her own. He always enjoyed how Margaret's fur felt against his skin. She liked this, too. He smiled. She p u r r r r r e d.

"Good morning, *amore mio*," the Pope said. *Amore mio* is Italian. It means "my love."

"Today is *Maundy Thursday*," he added. *Maundy!?* *More strange words!* Margaret thought.

She wasn't sure that she was going to like everything that was happening this week. . . .

CHAPTER 2

Just then, there was a knock on the door of the apartment. *Is it food?* Margaret wondered. Margaret is always hungry when she wakes up.

"Come in!" the Pope called out from across the room.

In walked a man with a tray, and on the tray, much to Margaret's delight, were several of her favorite breakfast dishes.

She saw fresh, warm rolls, butter and jam, a cup of yogurt, and a much larger cup (it was really the size of a bowl) of *caffè latte*. That means warm coffee with milk.

Cats don't usually drink coffee, and they probably aren't supposed to, which is why the cooks in the Vatican know to make Margaret's morning latte with a whole lot of frothy milk and very little actual coffee.

Margaret grabbed a roll in one paw, and began to slurp the latte. While she slurped, some of it splashed onto the coffee table. Then, when she reached for the jam, to add it to her roll, her paw went right to the bottom of the little dish in which it was set. This meant that for a few minutes wherever Margaret walked there were jam paw-prints on the white carpet. The steward who had delivered the tray looked annoyed. The Pope just smiled.

The Pope said, "I want to show you my chapel, Margaret. Finish your breakfast."

So, she finished that roll, and quickly grabbed another, but when the jam was all gone, she lost interest. Lapping up the remaining bits of milky goodness in the saucer, she walked over to where the Pope was sitting in a chair by the window studying a stack of papers.

"Ready?" he said, and when Margaret purred back at him, he knew that she was. She still had froth on her whiskers.

Now, Vatican City, where Margaret and the Pope live, is situated on the banks of an ancient river: the Tiber. Not *tiger*—Margaret wouldn't like that! — but *Tiber*.

On the other side of the Tiber River from the Vatican is one of the most historic, ancient, and beautiful cities in the world: Rome. For more than 1,000 years, Rome was the center of Western civilization. Before there was a Vatican City, the Pope was the ruler of all of Rome, and beyond, including most of Italy, and even beyond Italy, of other countries in Europe. And when popes ruled these vast lands they hired famous artists to build beautiful churches, galleries for art, libraries, and chapels.

So off went Margaret and the Pope out of the apartment and down the stairs into a corridor. There were Swiss Guards all along the hallways as they walked side by side. Some of the guards stood at attention, as they usually do, without looking at Margaret. But one or two of them, who have taken a special liking to her, nodded or winked.

The Pope often visits this chapel, but I've never seen it, Margaret thought to herself.

As they approached, Margaret saw a line of people who looked like they were waiting to get in.

"The Sistine Chapel," a sign read, in front of them.

"Holy Father, the chapel doesn't open to tourists for another hour," one of the guards said to the Pope, adding, "Would you like more time than that?"

"No, that's fine, thank you, Michael. I only want to show Margaret around," the Pope replied.

As they walked across the threshold, Margaret's eyes became huge like the saucer that held her morning latte. She couldn't believe what she saw. She had never seen anything like this before on the streets of Rome. She hadn't seen anything like this, yet, in the Vatican, either.

Every inch of the walls and ceiling was painted with the most amazing pictures!

While Margaret began to take it all in, the Pope walked quietly to the front of the chapel and knelt on the stairs in front of the altar. *What is he doing?* Margaret wondered, but then she looked again at the walls, the ceiling.

She almost fell over backward, trying to see the paintings on the ceiling above her head. The ceiling in the Sistine Chapel is forty-four feet tall in the middle. That's as tall as seven or eight adults standing one on top of another!

Looking up, Margaret saw a huge man painted on the ceiling directly above her. The man was reaching out his finger and touching the finger of what looked like another, much older, man. Margaret didn't know it, then, but that picture is how the famous painter imagined God creating the first man, Adam, in the Garden of Eden.

Margaret looked again at the Pope. He was still there, kneeling in the front of the chapel. She walked over to where he was and placed her paws in front of her. His eyes were closed. Margaret looked carefully at him, and she began to think. A minute later, Margaret closed her eyes, too.

The Pope was praying. Do cats pray? I honestly don't know for sure, but it looked as if Margaret were praying too.

After a few minutes, the Pope opened his eyes and smiled at Margaret there beside him. He made the Sign of the Cross. Then he got back onto his feet. Margaret did, too.

As they walked out of the Sistine Chapel, the Pope explained: "Margaret, five hundred years ago Pope Julius II asked a great artist named Michelangelo to paint this ceiling. Fifteen thousand people will come through here today, as they do every day, to see these paintings."

CHAPTER 3

As the Pope and Margaret emerged from the Sistine Chapel, some of the tourists who were waiting in line saw them come out, and they cheered. The Pope picked Margaret up in his arms and walked over to the crowd standing behind a long rope.

Margaret saw kids with parents, and people who appeared to be from all over the world. There were people with brown skin, tan skin, white skin, and black skin. Together, Margaret and the Pope began to greet each person, one at a time.

Adults were reaching out to the Pope to touch his hands, and children were reaching for Margaret, wanting to hug her.

This lasted only a few minutes, however, because then three of the Pope's secretaries came rushing up and said, "There is so much to do, Holy Father. We need you to come to the office to discuss the plans for today."

Then, Father Felipe appeared. Father Felipe works very closely with the Pope on the details of his work each day.

"Allow me to return Margaret to our apartment, and then I'll be right with you," the Pope said to Felipe. Felipe nodded. "Of course, Holy Father," he said.

Then Felipe and the others accompanied Margaret and the Pope back down the corridor and up the stairs.

Once they returned to the apartment, Margaret heard Father Felipe say, "There is so much to do before we go to the prison this afternoon. . . ." And then, suddenly, he and the Pope were leaving the room, walking out into the hallway.

Wait a minute. The prison?! Oh my! Margaret thought.

She was worried again. She had to do something.

What Margaret did not yet know, was that Maundy Thursday is the day in Holy Week when we remember Jesus washing the feet of his disciples. When Jesus began to wash their feet, like a servant who takes care of his master, Jesus shocked his friends, the disciples.

They told him that he shouldn't wash their feet.

But Jesus insisted. He said, "If I . . . the master and teacher, have washed your feet, you ought to wash one another's feet. I have given you a model to follow, so that as I have done for you, you should also do."

That's why Christians wash each other's feet on Maundy Thursday. And that's why the Pope was going to a Roman prison that afternoon: to wash the feet of prisoners, showing them, and anyone else who might be watching, that a Pope is a follower of Jesus, and a servant to other people.

But Margaret didn't know any of that. Not yet. And when Margaret is worried, she doesn't usually sit still. So as soon as the Pope and Father Felipe left the apartment, leaving Margaret behind, she tried running after them.

She made it as far as the hallway, past the Swiss Guard, who pretended not to notice, but she slowed down to look at a painting on the wall of Jesus washing feet.

Then, she didn't know which way the Pope had gone. She had to choose from among four different stairways! She picked one, and ran down it, but before she knew it, Margaret realized she was standing in the kitchen.

The cooks had seen her coming.

"My little Margarita!" one of them called out. He was from Argentina, where people speak Spanish, and in Spanish, Margarita, which sounds a lot like Margaret, means "daisy flower."

Feeling at home right away, Margaret jumped up on a counter in the middle of the kitchen. The cooks were just then preparing lunch, and since Holy Week is during Lent, they were not preparing meat. To some people, this may sound difficult or disappointing, but to Margaret, it only meant more fish. And Margaret loves fish!

Margaret forgot all about the Pope, the prison, and everything else. She was suddenly hungry again.

Two platefuls later, Margaret was still there on the kitchen counter, busily licking herself clean.

"My, what an appetite!" the cooks were saying, and, "I can't believe it, she eats so much!"

It was about then that Margaret began to feel sleepy. While the cooks were cleaning up from lunch, Margaret found a corner and settled herself on top of a large burlap sack full of potatoes. She liked the earthy smell of the potatoes and the sack. It reminded her of the Via della Conciliazione, where she had once lived.

Within a few minutes, Margaret fell asleep.

The Pope, meanwhile, had finished his work and was back to the apartment with Father Felipe, preparing to leave for the prison. "Has anyone seen Margaret?" he asked, looking around the room.

Father Felipe and a steward shook their heads, no. But, just then, the cook who called her "Margarita" carried Margaret through the door in his arms.

"Holy Father," the cook said, "Margarita had lunch in the kitchen with us. Then, she fell asleep."

"I hope she didn't cause too much trouble . . .," the Pope said.

"Not at all, Holy Father," the cook promised, as he passed Margaret from his arms to the Pope's.

Margaret was awake again by the time she and the Pope and Father Felipe were in the car driving out of the Vatican. They didn't have far to travel.

When they arrived at the prison, Margaret watched as the Pope talked to the small audience for a while and then as he knelt, as he had done in Sistine Chapel, in front of each man in prisoner clothing, carefully washing his feet with warm water.

Everyone was very quiet while the Pope did this. Margaret noticed that some of the men were crying softly, but they were smiling, too.

Margaret followed the Pope, standing at his side each time that he knelt.

She was nervous and uncomfortable at first, not sure what she should do.

But by the time the Pope came to the last man, and began to wash his feet, Margaret knew.

She watched as the Pope washed the last man's feet, and the man leaned forward and kissed the Pope on his forehead. The Pope smiled back at him and said to him quietly, "*Mio fratello.*" That's Italian. It means "My brother." Then, Margaret leaned forward, feeling more confident now. She licked the man's feet. He smiled at her.

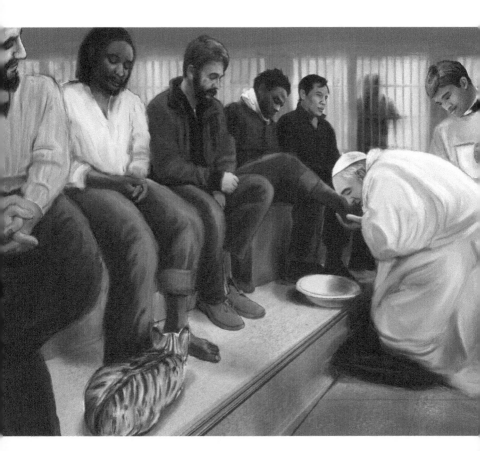

CHAPTER 4

The following morning, Margaret woke early. The sun was already coming up over the buildings. She knew that this day was Good Friday and that is when we remember and honor Jesus, who died for us on the cross. That was such an awful thing that Jesus had to do, and yet we call it "Good" Friday. Margaret paused and thought about this.

She knew the Pope would be busy today. Even though she had woken up early, looking around the apartment she could see that he was already gone. He was probably at Mass.

A few minutes later, he walked into the room and announced:

"Today, Margaret, we remember Our Lord and his death." Then, he picked her up in his arms and added, "Good morning, sweetness." He kissed her on her cheek where her whiskers are. It tickled.

Margaret felt happy. She looked in his eyes.

"Do you see all of the people outside?" the Pope said, gesturing to the window. He set her down on the table by the window to look.

It was a familiar sight to Margaret, as she looked down into St. Peter's Square and saw thousands of pilgrims who had come to Rome and the Vatican for this Holy Week, for this holy day.

"They have come to celebrate the Passion of Our Lord and to walk the 𝔙ia 𝔠rucis with us," the Pope said.

There was that word again, "Passion." Margaret was beginning to understand that it meant the suffering and pain Jesus had to undergo for us during the first Holy Week about 2,000 years ago.

𝔙ia 𝔠rucis means the Way of the Cross. The Pope said, "This evening, for the 𝔙ia 𝔠rucis, I will take you to the Roman Colosseum."

Margaret jumped down from the table. She looked up at him as if to say, *To the what? Where?*

"The Colosseum is the place here in Rome where, in the years after Jesus died on the cross at the hands of the Romans, the Roman Empire went on to kill many of Jesus's followers."

Margaret suddenly looked frightened.

"We'll be safe," the Pope assured her. "Romans don't kill Christians today. That was long ago."

Margaret's mind then turned to the subject of breakfast. All she saw on a tray on the coffee table was a bowl of fruit and some cereal. She began to look around the room. Maybe she had slept while the stewards came in, and missed the tasty things. She went to the door and looked around the corner. There was no sign of anything else, not anywhere.

"We are fasting today, sweetness," the Pope said, noticing her search. "I asked them for a very simple breakfast and lunch. We can eat light, to honor Our Lord who suffered much."

A few hours later, when the Pope left to preside over another Mass in St. Peter's Basilica, Margaret snuck down the hall, down the stairs, and through the corridor, to join him.

At Mass, the Pope didn't know Margaret was there, but that was okay, because Margaret remembered St. Peter's from the day she had spent in the Basilica not long ago on Christmas Eve. In the nave of the huge church, she found an out-of-the-way corner. She listened to the Mass from there.

Margaret sat near an older woman who had a guide dog beside her. Margaret and the dog made easy friends.

From where she sat, Margaret could hear the Pope as he preached his homily, and she watched him closely as he did something unusual. She saw the Pope lie flat on his face and belly, prostrate on the marble floor. This, she learned later, was in humble obedience and honor to God on this passion-filled day. Margaret had never seen him do that before.

When Father Felipe came, later that day, to tell the Pope it was time to go the Colosseum, Felipe was worried when the Pope said Margaret was coming too.

"Of course she is coming," the Pope said, and then added, "Margaret is experiencing so many things during this, her first Holy Week." He winked at her.

A few moments later, the Pope picked Margaret up and tucked her inside his cassock. Together, they followed Felipe to the car.

CHAPTER 5

The following morning was Holy Saturday, a very quiet day in the Vatican.

But that evening was the Easter Vigil in St. Peter's Basilica, which ended at midnight, and then it was Easter Sunday! Margaret knew that Easter is the day we celebrate Jesus's coming back to life. Easter

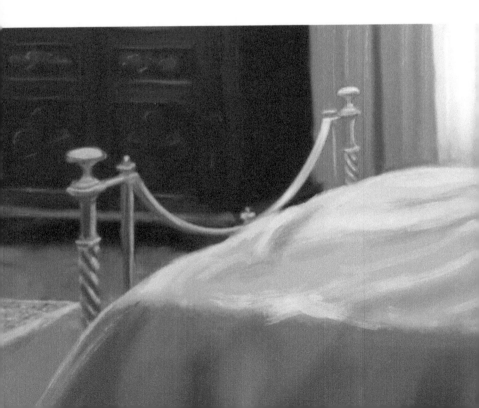

means that Holy Week is over. Jesus shows us what resurrection means.

That Sunday morning, bells were ringing in the Vatican and in all the churches of Rome. Margaret could hear those joyful bells, but it wasn't the bells that woke her up. She was up at dawn, ready to go.

The Pope gave her a look of surprise when he saw her standing at his feet before he had even gotten out of bed. "Darling Margaret! My, my, you are up and ready for this special day, aren't you?" he said.

She looked at him and smiled.

"Christ is risen!" the Pope said. At that moment, Father Felipe walked into the room. "Excuse me, Holy Father, I was coming in to be sure you were awake. Big day today!"

"Margaret already woke me up, Felipe, but thank you," the Pope said.

Then he turned back to face Margaret. He whispered to her, "You know what we're going to do tonight to celebrate?"

Margaret looked at him with anticipation.

"We're going to ask the cooks to make us some pizza!" he said. "Not just any pizza—*Pizza a Caballo.*"

If you didn't grow up speaking Spanish, you might not know what that means.

A caballo means "on horseback" because *Pizza a Caballo* has something extra—a piece of delicious flatbread on top. It's like eating a pizza sandwich!

Margaret p u r r r r r e d and licked her lips.

When the Pope was dressed, he picked up Margaret and opened the door to the apartment.

There, in the hallway, waiting patiently, were Father Felipe and some other members of the Curia.

Two Swiss Guards were also there, waiting to escort them down the stairs and onto the balcony where the Pope would give a special Easter greeting to a huge crowd that had gathered in St. Peter's Square.

What exactly is going to happen, next? Margaret wondered. She thought about this while they walked down the stairs.

"*Urbi et orbi,*" said the Pope, as they headed toward the open doors and the crowd below.

"You remember this, don't you, Margaret?"

By now, there were a few secretaries running beside them, as well. It seemed to Margaret as if there were people hurrying everywhere.

The Pope picked Margaret up. "*Urbi et orbi,* my dear. Remember? It is time for me to speak to the City and to the World."

"What do you think I should say?" he whispered gently in her ear.

Margaret thought. She pondered all that she had experienced during her first Holy Week. Then, she thought about Easter. She wanted to keep on thinking, but suddenly the Pope set her down on the balcony beside him. Margaret could see thousands of people in the Square below. She watched as the Pope approached the microphone that was there. Then, she heard the crowd begin to cheer.

THE END

ABOUT THE AUTHOR

Jon M. Sweeney is an author, husband, and father of four. He has been interviewed on many television programs including CBS Saturday Morning, Fox News, and PBS's Religion and Ethics Newsweekly. His popular history *The Pope Who Quit: A True Medieval Tale of Mystery, Death, and Salvation* has been optioned by HBO and may soon be developed into a film. He's the author of thirty-five other books, including *The Complete Francis of Assisi, When Saint Francis Saved the Church*, the winner of an award in history from the Catholic Press Association, and *The Enthusiast: How the Best Friend of Francis of Assisi Almost Destroyed What He Started*. This is his third book for children. He presents often at literary and religious conferences, and churches, writes regularly for *America* in the US and *The Tablet* in the UK, and is active on social media (Twitter @ jonmsweeney; Facebook jonmsweeney).

ABOUT THE ILLUSTRATOR

Roy DeLeon is an Oblate of St. Benedict, a spiritual director, a workshop facilitator focused on creative praying, an Urban Sketcher, and a professional illustrator. In addition to illustrating *The Pope's Cat* series, he is also the author of *Praying with the Body: Bringing the Psalms to Life*. He lives in Bothell, Washington, with his wife, Annie.

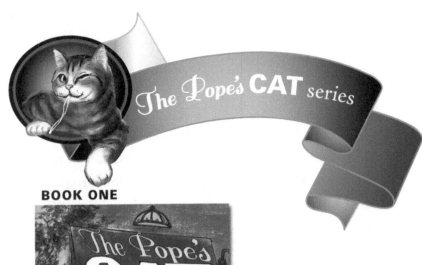

The Pope's CAT series

BOOK ONE

ISBN 978-1-61261-935-4
$9.99

In case you're wondering how the Pope and Margaret first met . . .

This is the book where it all started—the story of Margaret when she was a stray cat on the Via della Conciliazione in Rome, and how she was adopted by the Pope and then began running the Vatican from museum to floorboard.

BOOK TWO

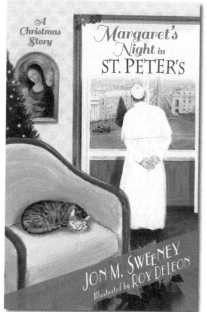

ISBN 978-1-61261-936-1
$10.99

In this delightful new story from their lives, the Pope takes Margaret on a tour of St. Peter's. But when he's called away to work, Margaret becomes lost in the world's largest church. She meets saints, children, tourists, and the artist Michelangelo's famous statue, The Pietà, before being reunited with the Pope as Midnight Mass is about to begin.

COMING IN Spring 2020

Margaret AND THE POPE
Go to Assisi

BOOK FOUR

ISBN 978-1-61261-935-4
$9.99

"Where is she?" said the Vatican's director of television broadcasting, as he walked into the Pope's outer office. "Where did she go?" He sounded a little bit angry.

"Who is that, Father?" Father Felipe said.

"His Holiness's cat!" replied the director.

"Has something happened involving Margaret?" Felipe inquired. But he knew what was probably happening— Margaret had gotten herself into trouble. Again.

"We were broadcasting the Pope's Wednesday general audience when that cat started rubbing her head against one of the speakers. Then, she ran up to His Holiness, interrupting his homily. Oh, it was awful!" the director said.

Felipe smiled.

He knew what the Pope would say, and he knew exactly where Margaret would be hiding. . . .